Lost in the Roses

Written & Illustrated by Marina Valentina

red
cygnet®
PRESS

San Diego, California

red cygnet® PRESS

To everyone and everything that came my way. – M.V.

Illustrations copyright © 2008 Marina Valentina
Manuscript copyright © 2008 Marina Valentina
Book copyright © 2008 Red Cygnet Press, Inc., 11858 Stoney Peak Dr. #525, San Diego, CA 92128

Cover and book design: Amy Stirnkorb

First Edition 2008
10 9 8 7 6 5 4 3 2
Printed in China

Library of Congress Cataloging-in-Publication Data

Valentina, Marina.
Lost in the roses / written and illustrated by Marina Valentina. -- 1st ed.
p. cm.
Summary: A chick falls asleep in a giant rose and has a magical adventure in the sparkly skies.
ISBN 978-1-60108-014-1
[1. Chickens--Fiction. 2. Roses--Fiction.] I. Title.
PZ7.V2332Lo 2008
[E]--dc22
2006036768

Early one morning a young chick lay in the tall grass.
Soon, she became restless.

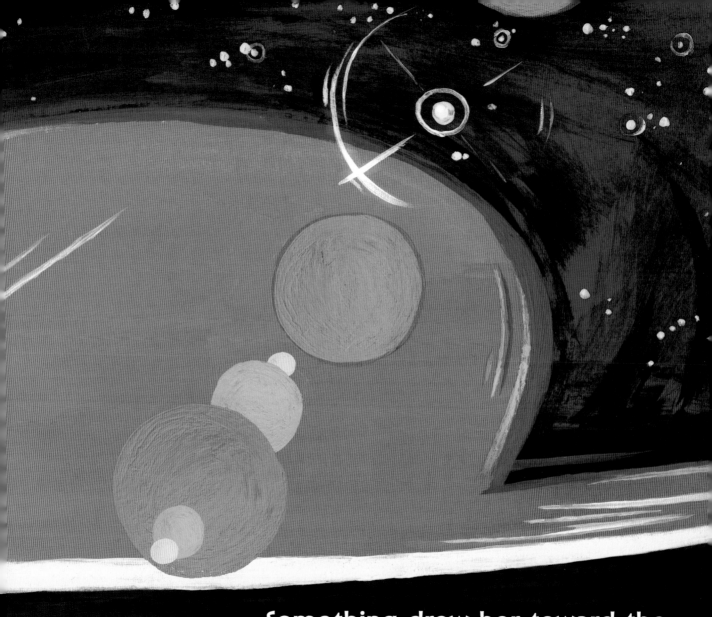

Something drew her toward the
twinkle of the stars. She followed them for
hours and hours, until the sun rose

By morning, the stars had gone away.
Now, the chick could not find her way home.

The chick found
herself lost in a field
of giant roses.

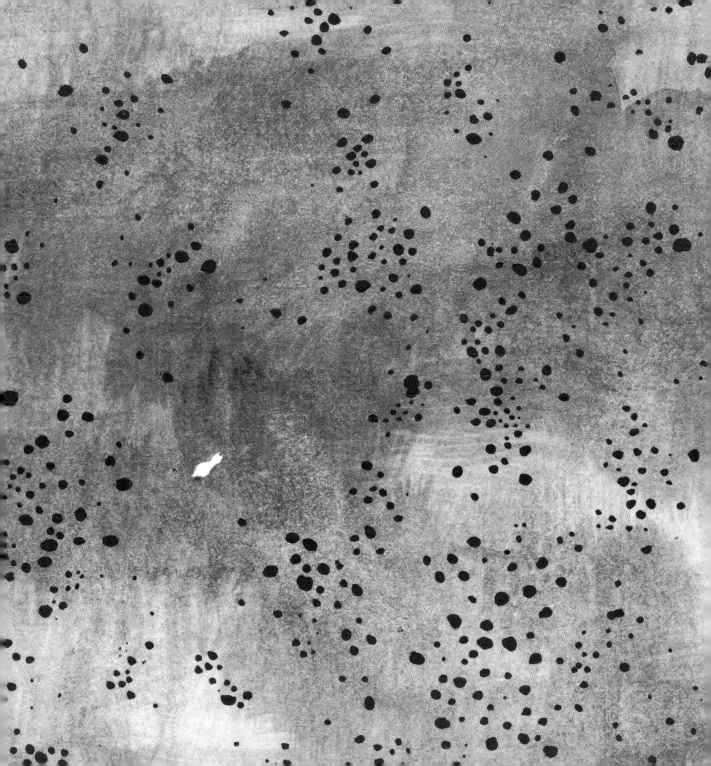

As night fell, she watched the sun paint the sky.

It felt good to curl up in a big rose...

...and dream rosy dreams.

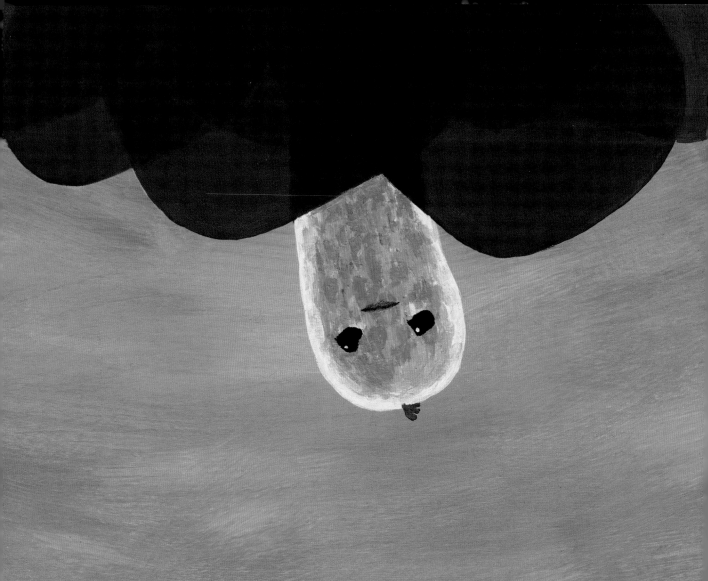

By the next morning, the chick
realized the roses had risen to
higher and higher heights!

The thorns frightened the chick. She imagined what might happen to her if she jumped.

She felt there was nothing left to do, and nothing left to think. Her mind became blank.

With all her thoughts and worries gone,
she finally saw the beauty of it all...

As she admired the view, the chick noticed a petal fall gently to the ground.

She had an idea!

She climbed onto a petal, and caught a sparkle in the distance. The sparkle drew her in. Wherever she looked, the petal would go.

Soon, the chick
saw her friends far
away in the distance!
She could not wait
to hug them all.

That night, they all snuggled
under the rosy petal. Her friends
listened with wonder as the
chick shared all she had done,
and all she had learned
on her magical journey.

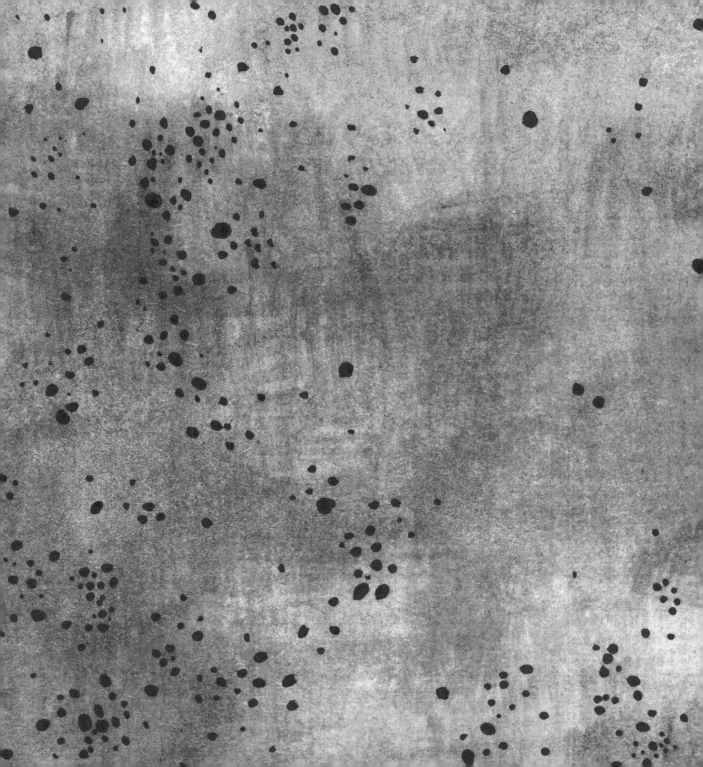